Night
LIGHTS
for Students

S0-AQF-087

New Leaf Press

First Printing: March 2004

Copyright © 2004 by New Leaf Press, Inc. All rights
reserved. No part of this book may be reproduced in
any manner whatsoever without written permission of
the publisher, except in the case of brief quotations in
articles and reviews. For information write: New Leaf
Press, Inc., P.O. Box 726, Green Forest, AR 72638.

Cover and interior design by Brent Spurlock
Edited by Jim Fletcher and Roger Howerton

ISBN: 0-89221-571-2
Library of Congress Catalog Card Number:
2003116016

Please visit our web site for more great titles:
www.newleafpress.net

New Leaf Press

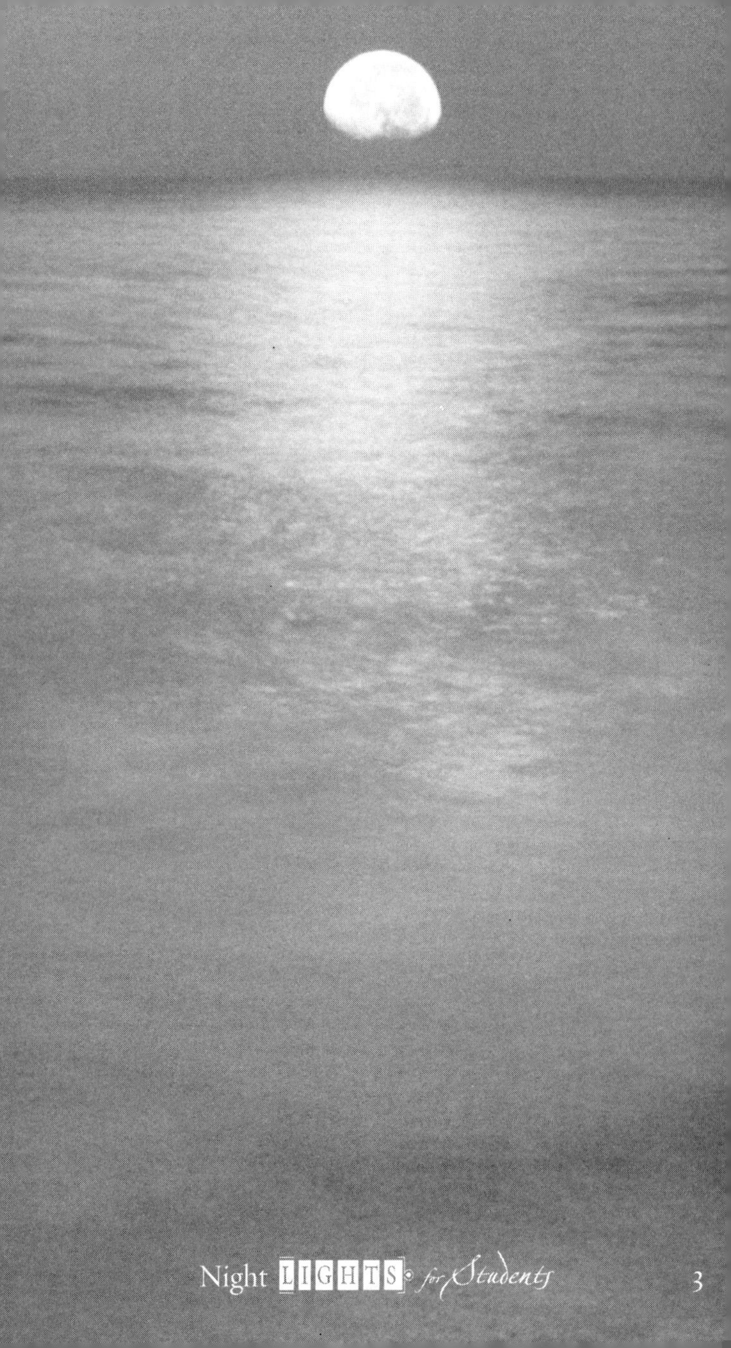

A special gift for you

To

_____

From

_____

T he local sheriff was looking for a deputy, and one of the applicants — who was not known to be the brightest academically, was called in for an interview. "Okay," began the sheriff, "What is 1 and 1?"

"Eleven," came the reply. The sheriff thought to himself, *That's not what I meant, but he's right.*

Then the sheriff asked, "What two days of the week start with the letter *t* ?"

"Today & tomorrow," replied the applicant. The sheriff was again surprised over the answer, one that he had never thought of himself.

"Now, listen carefully. Who killed Abraham Lincoln?" asked the sheriff.

The job seeker seemed a little surprised, then thought really hard for a minute and finally admitted, "I don't know."

The sheriff replied, "Well, why don't you go home and work on that one for a while?"

The applicant left and wandered over to his pals who were waiting to hear the results of the interview. He greeted them with a cheery smile, "The job is mine! The interview went great! First day on the job and I'm already working on a murder case!"

TODAY ...

TOMORROW ...

Write down your thoughts, dreams, and hopes.

> Whatsoever thy hand findeth to do, do it with thy might.
>
> — Ecclesiastes 9:10

Whenever you are asked if you can do a job, tell 'em, Certainly I can! — and get busy and find out how to do it.

— Theodore Roosevelt

W hen I was a kid, adults used to bore me to tears with their tedious diatribes about how hard things were when they were growing up. What with walking twenty-five miles to school every morning, uphill both ways through year-round blizzards, carrying their younger siblings on their backs to their one-room schoolhouse where they maintained a straight-A average; despite their full-time after-school job at the local textile mill where they worked for 35 cents an hour just to help keep their family from starving to death!

And I remember promising myself that when I grew up there was no way I was going to say stuff like that about how hard I had it and how easy they've got it! But ... now that I've reached the ripe old age of 29, I can't help but look around and notice the youth of today. You've got it so easy!

I mean, compared to my childhood, you live in Utopia! And I hate to say it, but you kids today — you don't know how good you've got it!

I mean, when I was a kid we didn't have the Internet. If we wanted to know something, we had to go to the library and look it up ourselves! And there was no e-mail! We had to actually write somebody a letter with a pen! — and then you had to walk all the way across the street and put it in the mailbox and it would take like a week to get there!

And there were no MP3s or Napsters! You wanted to steal music, you had to go to the record store and shoplift it yourself! Or we had to wait around all day to tape it off the radio and the DJ'd usually talk over the beginning and you'd have to do it all over again!

You want to hear about hardship?

We didn't have call waiting! If you were on the phone and somebody else called, they got a busy signal! And we didn't have fancy caller ID boxes either! When the phone rang, you had no idea who it was. It could be your boss, your mom, a collections agent — you didn't know!!! You just had to pick it up and take your chances, mister!

And we didn't have any fancy Sony Playstation videogames with high-resolution 3-D graphics! We had the Atari 2600! With games like "Space Invaders" and "Asteroids." Your guy was a little square! You had to use your imagination! And there were no multiple levels or screens, it was just one screen forever! And you could never win, the game just kept getting harder and faster until you died! Just like LIFE!

When you went to the movie theater, there was no such thing as stadium seating! All the seats were the same height! If a tall guy sat in front of you, you were out of luck!

And sure, we had cable television, but back

then that was only like 20 channels and there was no on-screen menu! You had to use a little book called a *TV Guide* to find out what was on! And there was no Cartoon Network! You could only get cartoons on Saturday morning. D'ya hear what I'm saying!?! We had to wait ALL WEEK, you spoiled little brats! That's exactly what I'm talking about!

You kids today have got it too easy! You're spoiled, I swear! You guys wouldn't have lasted five minutes back in 1987!

Today ...

Tomorrow...

Write down your thoughts, dreams, and hopes.

> *Do all things without murmurings and disputings.*
> — Philippians 2:14

When I was a boy of fourteen, my father was so ignorant I could hardly stand to have the old man around. But when I got to be twenty-one, I was astonished at how much the old man had learned in seven years.

— Mark Twain

THE ATTITUDE CHANGE

Bruce Larson tells this story in his book, *Faith for the Journey*. Once there was a successful factory that made drills. One day the owner told his corporate officials that he was going to retire and that he had chosen his son as his successor. At the next board meeting, the son asked his four vice presidents, "What are your goals for the company for the next five to ten years?"

One vice-president replied, "Well sir, we're looking at new sizes and shapes for different drills."

The son then dropped his bombshell. "I have news for you. There is no market for drills." One could feel the tension in the air. He continued, "From now on we will not think drills. We will not sell drills. We'll sell holes! People don't want to buy a drill; they want to make a hole!"

As they began to think of other ways to create holes, they developed, among other methods, lasers for hole drilling. This attitude change and other innovations keep this company in business while its competitors lost large shares of the market and some even went bankrupt.[1]

TODAY ...

TOMORROW ...

Write down your thoughts, dreams, and hopes.

> Create in me a clean heart, O God; and renew a right spirit within me.
>
> – Psalm 51:10

There's more than one way

to skin a cat.

— American proverb

The Best OFFENSE Is a Good Defense

In late September 1864, Confederate General Nathan Bedford Forrest was leading his troops north from Decatur, Alabama, toward Nashville. But to make it to Nashville, Forrest would have to defeat the Union Army at Athens, Alabama. When the Union commander, Colonel Wallace Campbell, refused to surrender, Forrest asked for a personal meeting, and took Campbell on an inspection of his troops.

But each time they left a detachment, the Confederate soldiers simply packed up and moved to another position, artillery and all. Forrest and Campbell would then arrive at the new encampment and continue to tally up the impressive number of Confederate soldiers and weaponry. By the time they returned to the fort, Campbell was convinced he couldn't win and surrendered unconditionally.[2]

TODAY ...

_____

_____

_____

_____

_____

_____

_____

_____

_____

_____

TOMORROW ...

_____

_____

_____

_____

Write down your thoughts, dreams, and hopes.

Or what king, going to make war against another king, sitteth not down first, and consulteth whether he be able with ten thousand to meet him that cometh against him with twenty thousand?

– Luke 14:31

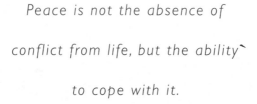

Peace is not the absence of conflict from life, but the ability to cope with it.

– Anonymous

SCARS OF A BAD TEMPER

There once was a little boy who had a bad temper. His father gave him a bag of nails and told him that every time he lost his temper, he must hammer a nail into the back of the fence.

The first day, the boy had driven 37 nails into the fence.

Over the next few weeks, as he learned to control his anger, the number of nails hammered daily gradually dwindled down. He discovered it was easier to hold his temper than to drive those nails into the fence.

Finally the day came when the boy didn't lose his temper at all. He told his father about it and the father suggested that the boy now pull out one nail for each day that he was able to hold his temper.

The days passed and the young boy was finally able to tell his father that all the nails were gone.

The father took his son by the hand and led him to the fence.

He said, "You have done well, my son, but look at the holes in the fence. The fence will never be the same. When you say things in anger, they leave a scar just like this one. You can put a knife in a man and draw it out. It won't matter how many times you say 'I'm sorry,' the wound is still there."

$\mathbf{T}$ODAY ...

$\mathbf{T}$OMORROW ...

Write down your thoughts, dreams, and hopes.

> *For the wrath of man worketh not the*
> *righteousness of God.*
>
> *— James 1:20*

It is the great duty of all

Christians to put off anger.

— Philip Henry

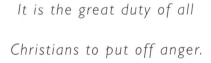

A church had appointed a committee to search for a new pastor. The committee received the following letter of application:

I understand your church is looking for a pastor. I should like to submit my application. I am generally considered to be a good preacher. I have been a leader in most of the places I have served. I have also found time to do some writing on the side. I am over fifty years of age, and while my health is not the best, I still manage to get enough work done to please my congregation.

As for a reference, I am somewhat handicapped. I have never served in any place more than three years, and the churches where I have preached have generally been pretty small, even though they were located in rather large cities. Some places I had to leave because my ministry caused riots and disturbances. When I stayed, I did not get along too well with other religious leaders in town which may influence the kind of references these places will send you. I have also been threatened several times and been physically attacked. Three or four times I have gone to jail for expressing my thoughts. You will need to know that there are some men who follow me around undermining my work. Still, I feel sure I can bring vitality to your church. If you can use me, I should be pleased to be considered.

The committee was dismayed that anyone would think that its church could use such a man. A trouble-making, absent-minded, ex-jailbird could not possibly be an effective pastor, let alone be accepted by the community.

"What was his name?" they asked.

The chairman of the committee said, "I do not know. The letter is simply signed, 'Paul'."

Today ...

Tomorrow ...

Write down your thoughts, dreams, and hopes.

And he said unto me, My grace is sufficient for thee: for my strength is made perfect in weakness. Most gladly therefore will I rather glory in my infirmities, that the power of Christ may rest upon me.

– 2 Corinthians 12:9

You can't lead anyone else further

than you have gone yourself.

– Gene Mauch

PONDERABLES

hy does the sun lighten our hair, but darken our skin?

Why can't women put on mascara with their mouth closed?

Why don't you ever see the headline "Psychic Wins Lottery"?

Why is "abbreviated" such a long word?

Why is it that doctors call what they do "practice"?

Why is lemon juice made with artificial flavor, and dishwashing liquid made with real lemons?

Why is the man who invests all your money called a broker?

Why is the time of day with the slowest traffic called rush hour?

Why isn't there mouse-flavored cat food?

When dog food is new and improved tasting, who tests it?

Why didn't Noah swat those two mosquitoes?

Why do they sterilize the needle for lethal injections?

You know that indestructible black box that is used on airplanes? Why don't they make the whole plane out of that stuff?

Why don't sheep shrink when it rains?

Why are they called apartments when they are all stuck together?

If con is the opposite of pro, is congress the opposite of progress?

If flying is so safe, why do they call the airport the terminal? [3]

Today ...

Tomorrow ...

Write down your thoughts, dreams, and hopes.

> But foolish and unlearned questions avoid,
> knowing that they do gender strifes.
> — 2 Timothy 2:23

To think is an effort; to think rightly

is a great effort, and to think as

a Christian ought to think is the

greatest effort of a human soul.

— Oswald Chambers

IDENTITY CRISIS

A test is a difficult experience through which a person's true values, commitments and beliefs are revealed. A college sophomore in anticipation of a notoriously difficult final exam in his ornithology class made what he considered the ultimate effort in preparation for the exam. He was then stunned when he walked into the classroom to take the exam. There was no blue book, no multiple-choice questions, no text booklet at all — just 25 pictures on the wall. The test was to identify birds from the photos — photos not of birds, but of birds' feet.

"This is insane," the student protested. "It can't be done."

"It must be done," said the professor. "This is the final."

"I won't do it," the boy said. "I'm walking out."

"If you walk out, you will fail the final."

"Go ahead and fail me," the boy said, heading for the door.

"Okay, you have failed. What is your name?" the professor demands.

The boy pulled up his pants legs, kicked off his shoes and said, "You tell me!"

TODAY ...

TOMORROW ...

Write down your thoughts, dreams, and hopes.

> Blessed is the man who endures trial, for when he has stood the test he will receive the crown of life which God has promised to those who love him.
>
> – James 1:12

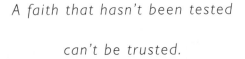

A faith that hasn't been tested

can't be trusted.

– Adrian Rogers

INTESTINAL FORTITUDE

K en Walker writes in *Christian Reader* that in the 1995 college football season 6-foot-2-inch, 280-pound Clay Shiver, who played center for the Florida State Seminoles, was regarded as one of the best in the nation. In fact, one magazine wanted to name him to their preseason all-America football team. But that was a problem, because the magazine was *Playboy*, and Clay Shiver is a dedicated Christian.

Shiver and the team chaplain suspected that *Playboy* would select him, and so he had time to prepare his response. Shiver knew well what a boon this could be for his career. Being chosen for this all-America team meant that sportswriters regarded him as the best in the nation at his position. Such publicity never hurts athletes who aspire to the pros and to multimillion-dollar contracts.

But Shiver had higher values and priorities. When informed that *Playboy* had made him their

selection, Clay shiver simply said, "No thanks."
That's right, he flatly turned down the honor.

"Clay didn't want to embarrass his mother
and grandmother by appearing in the magazine
or give old high school friends an excuse to buy
that issue," writes Walker. Shiver further explained
by quoting Luke 12:48: "To whom much is given,
of him much is required."

"I don't want to let anyone down," said Shiver,
"and number one on that list is God." [4]

TODAY ...

TOMORROW ...

Write down your thoughts, dreams, and hopes.

> Judge me, O LORD; for I have walked in mine integrity: I have trusted also in the LORD; therefore I shall not slide.
>
> – Psalm 26:1

God wants to develop the same

character traits in us as exist in

Christ. We are to react to the

situations of life as Christ did.

– Erwin W. Lutzer

im Bowden, in his book *One Crowded Hour* about cameraman Neil Davis, tells about an incident that happened in Borneo during the confrontination between Malaysia and Indonesia in 1964.

A group of Gurkhas from Nepal were asked if they would be willing to jump from transport planes into combat against the Indonesians if the need arose. The Gurkhas had the right to turn down the request because they had never been trained as paratroopers. Bowden quotes Davis's account of the story:

"Now the Gurkhas usually agreed to anything, but on this occasion, they provisionally rejected the plan. But the next day, one of their NCOs sought out the British officer who made the request and said they had discussed the matter further and would be prepared to jump under certain conditions.

"What are they?" asked the British officer.

"The Gurkhas told him they would jump if the land was marshy or reasonably soft with no rocky outcrops, because they were inexperienced in falling. The British officer considered this, and said that the dropping area would almost certainly be over jungle, and there would not be rocky outcrops, so that seemed all right. Was there anything else?

" 'Yes,' said the Gurkhas. They wanted the plane to fly as slowly as possible and no more than 100 feet high. The British officer pointed out the planes always fly as slowly as possible when dropping troops, but to jump from 100 feet was impossible, because the parachutes would not open in time from that height.

" 'Oh,' said the Gurkhas, 'that's all right, then. We'll jump with parachutes anywhere. You didn't mention parachutes before!' " [5]

T ODAY ...

T OMORROW ...

Write down your thoughts, dreams, and hopes.

> *But I wholly followed the LORD my God.*
> *— Joshua 14:8*

God does not so much need people

to do extraordinary things as He

needs people who do ordinary

things extraordinarily well.

— William Barclay

THE WHISPER TEST

In *The Whisper Test*, Mary Ann Bird writes:

I grew up knowing I was different, and I hated it. I was born with a cleft palate, and when I started school, my classmates made it clear to me how I looked to others: a little girl with a misshapen lip, crooked nose, lopsided teeth, and garbled speech.

When schoolmates asked, "What happened to your lip?" I'd tell them I'd fallen and cut it on a piece of glass. Somehow it seemed more acceptable to have suffered an accident than to have been born different. I was convinced that no one outside my family could love me.

There was, however a teacher in the second grade that we all adored — Mrs. Leonard by name. She was short, round, happy — a sparkling lady.

Annually we had a hearing test. . . .

Mrs. Leonard gave the test to everyone in the class, and finally it was my turn. I knew from past years that as we stood against the door and covered one ear, the teacher sitting at her desk would whisper something, and we would have to repeat it back — little things like "the sky is blue" or "do you have new shoes?" I waited there for those words that God must have put into her mouth, those seven words that changed my life. Mrs. Leonard said, in her whisper, "I wish you were my little girl."

God says to every person deformed by sin, "I wish you were my son" or "I wish you were my daughter." [6]

TODAY ...

TOMORROW ...

Write down your thoughts, dreams, and hopes.

> For God so loved the world, that he gave his only begotten Son, that whosoever believeth in him should not perish, but have everlasting life.
>
> – John 3:16

God did not choose us because we

were worthy, but by choosing us,

He makes us worthy.

— *Thomas Watson*

KEEPER OF THE SPRING

An elderly, quiet forest dweller once lived high above an Austrian village along the eastern slope of the Alps. Many years ago, the town council had hired this old gentleman as Keeper of the Spring to maintain the purity of the pools of water in the mountain crevices. The overflow from these pools ran down the mountainside and fed the lovely spring which flowed through the town. With faithful, silent regularity, the Keeper of the Spring patrolled the hills, removed the leaves and branches from the pools, and wiped away the silt that would otherwise choke and contaminate the fresh flow of water.

By and by, the village became a popular attraction for vacationers. Graceful swans floated along the crystal-clear spring, the mill wheels of various businesses located near the water turned day and night, farmlands were naturally irrigated, and the view from restaurants sparkled. Years passed. One evening the town council met for its semiannual meeting.

As the council members reviewed the budget, one man's eye caught the salary paid the obscure Keeper of the Spring. "Who is this old man?" he asked indignantly. "Why do we keep paying him year after year? No one ever sees him. For all we know, this man does us no good. He isn't necessary any longer!" By a unanimous vote, the council dispensed with the old man's services.

For several weeks, nothing changed. But by early autumn, the trees began to shed their leaves. Small branches snapped off and fell into the pools, hindering the rushing flow of sparkling water. One afternoon, someone noticed a slight yellowish-brown tint in the spring. A few days later, the water had darkened even more. Within a week, a slimy film covered sections of the water along the banks, and a foul odor emanated from the spring. The mill's wheels moved slowly; some finally ground to a halt. Businesses located near the water closed. The swans migrated to fresher waters far away, and tourists no longer visited the town. Eventually, the clammy fingers of disease and sickness reached deeply into the village.

The shortsighted town council enjoyed the beauty of the spring but underestimated the importance of guarding its source. We can make the same mistake in our lives. Like the Keeper of the Spring who maintained the purity of the water, you and I are the Keepers of Our Hearts. We need to consistently evaluate the purity of our hearts in prayer, asking God to reveal the little things that contaminate us. As God reveals our wrong attitudes, longings, and desires, we must remove them from our hearts.[7]

TODAY ...

TOMORROW ...

Write down your thoughts, dreams, and hopes.

> *Thy word have I hid in mine heart, that I*
> *might not sin against thee.*
>
> — Psalm 119:11

A heart in every thought renewed

And full of love divine,

Perfect and right and pure and good,

A copy, Lord, of thine.

— *Charles Wesley*

THE LOVE OF CHRIST

On the evening of April 25, 1958, a young Korean exchange student, a leader in student Christian affairs in the University of Pennsylvania, left his flat and went to the corner to post a letter to his parents in Pusan. Turning from the mailbox he stepped into the path of eleven leather-jacketed teenage boys. Without a word they attacked him, beating him with a blackjack, a lead pipe and with their shoes and fists. Later, when the police found him in the gutter, he was dead. All Philadelphia cried out for vengeance. The district attorney secured legal authority to try the boys as adults so that those found guilty could be given the death penalty. Then a letter arrived from Korea that made everyone stop and think. It was signed by the parents and by twenty other relatives of the murdered boy. It read in part:

"Our family has met together and we have

decided to petition that the most generous treatment possible within the laws of your government be given to those who have committed this criminal action. In order to give evidence of our sincere hope contained in this petition, we have decided to save money to start a fund to be used for the religious, educational, vocational, and social guidance of the boys when they are released. We have dared to express our hope with a spirit received from the gospel of our Savior Jesus Christ who died for our sins." [8]

TODAY ...

TOMORROW ...

Write down your thoughts, dreams, and hopes.

> Then said Jesus, Father, forgive them; for
> they know not what they do.
>
> — Luke 23:34

When you forgive, you in no way

change the past — but you sure

do change the future.

— Bernard Meltzer

CLEANUP

When a young man left his dorm and moved into an apartment, he went shopping for cleaning equipment. His cart was loaded with a broom, mop, dustpan, sponges and a full array of cleaning products. At the last minute he topped off his cart with a lone food purchase — a large bag of potato chips. Seeing the checkout clerk's quizzical look, he explained, "I'm a very messy eater."

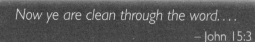

Now ye are clean through the word....
— John 15:3

TODAY …

_____

_____

_____

_____

_____

_____

_____

_____

TOMORROW …

_____

_____

_____

_____

_____

Write down your thoughts, dreams, and hopes.

QUALITY WORK

Here's how former Secretary of State Henry Kissinger, was able to inspire quality work. Once, he asked an assistant to prepare an analysis. The young man worked day and night on the project. An hour after he presented it to Kissinger, he got it back. There was a note attached that told him to redo it.

The assistant stayed up all night revising the report. Again, Kissinger asked him to redo it. After rewriting the report three times, the assistant asked to see Kissinger. He told him, "I've done the absolute best I can do."

Kissinger looked up and said, "In that case, I'll read it now." [9]

Be ye therefore perfect, even as your Father which is in heaven is perfect.
    – Matthew 5:48

TODAY ...

TOMORROW ...

Write down your thoughts, dreams, and hopes.

ARE YOU COLD YET?

I had to stop halfway home from work today to buy an ice scraper and some wiper fluid that wouldn't freeze when I used it. It was early November when the heater in my little Chevy pickup stopped working. That was actually the third heater I had installed in as many months and this time I opted to just bypass the system and go without its protection from the cold. I knew it would be freezing, but I assumed I could ride the winter out with the assistance of a couple blankets and some coffee. I almost made it, too.

There were a couple of late nights and some early morning drives that must have made me look pretty foolish. I had on several layers of clothing, a snowcap, and a hood. All of this was wrapped up in a blanket. Foolish looking I'm sure . . . but warm as a baby kangaroo in its mother's pouch.

As I said, I almost made it, but the inevitable

overlooked factor eventually came into play. You see, a little Chevy pickup without a heater is also a little Chevy pickup without any means to defrost the windshield.

Today was the first attempt I made to drive a long distance in freezing rain without the defrost working. The fog on the inside of the windshield wasn't that bad. I simply cracked the windows so that the both sides of the windshield were at the same 30-degree temperature. This eliminated the fog, but it didn't stop the ice from sticking to the outside of the glass.

Even the windshield wipers soon became ineffective as ice began to stick to ice. Add a little water from my wiper spray and the mess is complete. Thus, I had to stop halfway home from work today to buy an ice scraper and some wiper fluid that wouldn't freeze when I used it . . . so now you know why.

As I slowly made my way home, regularly spraying the windshield with antifreeze, the Lord took me back to my prayers this morning. The following is what I now find recorded in my journal.

"Lord, I'm really having a hard time. I can't really pinpoint it either. I lack whatever it is that causes people to become so devoted to You. Is it discipline or motivation . . . or am I lacking in something even greater, like true love or faith? Why is it so difficult to find consistency on a daily basis? How can a man, still attached to his flesh, find peace with God? How can he find consistency? If You show me, I'll tell the world."

My difficult drive home today was directly related to a decision I made three months ago. I foolishly believed that I could plow through winter on my own. "I don't need no stinkin' heater! I'm tough as nails." They say that hindsight is 20/20, and I believe them. Today, I can see three considerable flaws in my mindset last November.

1. "The heater isn't really that important."
2. "I'm tough enough to make it through the winter on my own."
3. "It will be easier to fix next summer anyway."

These three faulty views of reality are the same ones that affect my consistency with the Lord. Instead of a heater though, I assume that reading my Bible, prayer, accountably, or church aren't really that important. I also believe that I can make it through difficult trials on my own, leaving God out of the equation. Finally, I find that procrastination may be my biggest enemy yet. "I can read my Bible later." "I'll spend time in prayer right after I do this...." The list could go on forever.

Maybe you're like me. I've never actually expressed these ideas in thought or word, but they're evident in my lifestyle. If you're having a hard time discerning the truth within your own life, I challenge you to look for the warning signs.

1. Do you regularly make excuses for the decisions you've made in the past?
2. Are you overcompensating in other areas of life to make up for the missing consistency with God? (All those layers of clothing were really uncomfortable and restricting to my driving.)

3. Are you continually stopping on the side of the road in search of quick fixes to your problems?

4. Do you spend more time worrying about your bad decisions than you would have doing it God's way in the first place?

If you answered yes to any of these warning signs, I challenge you to commit to change. I have since realized how dangerous and stressful my decision to go without heat really was. In the same manner, the excuses that keep me from a consistent relationship with God are just as dangerous and stressful.

Do you want peace with God? Are you searching for a greater consistency in your relationship with Him? Maybe you need to go back a couple months and re-evaluate the decisions you've been making. After all, hindsight is 20/20 (Jeremiah 33:3; James 1:5).[10]

> *But seek ye first the kingdom of God, and his righteousness; and all these things shall be added unto you.*
>
> – Matthew 6:33

TODAY ...

TOMORROW ...

Write down your thoughts, dreams, and hopes.

CAST DOWN

Why are you cast down, O my soul?
And why are you disquieted within me?
Hope in God; for I shall yet praise Him,
the help of my countenance and my God.
- Psalm 42:11

It's easy to look back and see the places that I would so quickly want to forget and release from memory, and recognize what went wrong or at least how I could have coped in a better fashion. They are the places that were dark, not just dark enough where it was hard to see 20 feet in front of me, the ones that went pitch black. A place where my hope, my passion, and my purpose were severely challenged and significantly compromised. A place where regardless of what I tried to do, I was unable to get out. They are the places where I reluctantly admit that I was in some form, depressed.

I am not the type of person that readily admits my feelings. I have always managed to hold within myself emotions that so desperately want to get out. I am also the type of person that often tends to offer a personal challenge rather than a compassionate hug. In this struggle, depression, which in many cases feels as though it is the very struggle for oneself, I offer this hope: God truly wants you and desires you just as you are right now.

Weeping may endure for a night, but joy comes in the morning. – Psalm 30:5

Depression is a destructive element that can creep into our lives, and if left unchecked and unchallenged, can wreak havoc on our spiritual, emotional, and physical well-being. Most of us know this all too well from experience. It cannot only disrupt the way we interact with one another and our daily lives, it can affect the way in which we interact with our Lord and Savior. It is never a place we choose to be and always a place we want to leave. It is a far too easy place to fall into and a seemingly impossible place to climb out of. That is, when we attempt to climb on our own.

It's a lie!

Depression manages to deceive us from the inside out. Often it stems from a recognizable problem or situation, but many times it can quietly and slyly appear in our life. It can take many forms: distraction, anger, emotional distance, complacency, hopelessness, and defeat. It can speak many wounding lies: "you're alone, unwanted, useless, hopeless and lost." They are lies that speak counter to what God has spoken as truth.

It can shake the very core of what Our Lord established for us on the cross, but it was on that very cross that Christ defeated that which attempts to deceive us.

Yet it was our weaknesses he carried; it was our sorrows that weighed Him down. And we thought His troubles were a punishment from God for His own sins! But He was wounded and crushed for our sins. He was beaten that we might have peace. He was whipped and we were healed! All of us have strayed away like sheep. We have left God's path to follow our own. Yet the Lord laid on him the guilt and sins of us all.

— Isaiah 53:4-6

How can I find Him?

Overcoming depression is not always a simple fix. I am not a certified counselor, and do not profess to be one. I merely want to encourage you in the fundamentals of the faith in order to combat the destructive nature of this condition. We must first and always seek the power of God and His peace in a place of struggle.

But you O Lord are a shield for me, my glory and the One who lifts up my head. I cried to the Lord with my voice, and He heard me from His holy hill. I laid down and slept; I awoke for the Lord sustained me.

— Psalm 3:3-5

There are three simple principles in this passage that can practically guide us to the road of overcoming:

1) "But you O Lord are a shield for me, my glory and the One who lifts up my head." This passage instructs us to recognize the lordship of God in our lives. We must pursue and persist after God in times of depression. We must fervently defend the place that God has in our hearts and in our minds. We must do all that we can to defend the truth as it directly applies to us by reading and meditating on the Word of God.

2) "I cried to the Lord with my voice." Never stop asking Him for help. If you feel as though you have taken the last possible step you can take after Him, take one more. Please, reader, hear me (though I am also writing to myself), if you fail to continue chasing after the Lord when you are in a place of desperate need, you will never find your way out.

3) "I laid down and slept; I awoke for the Lord had sustained me." You must rest. Depression is

not overcome by activity, being merely put aside for another time. Jesus has called those who are weary and heavy laden, promising rest for their souls. We are called to rest in the promise of His Word. What can this practically mean? Take time for just you and God and the desires He has placed on your heart.

Depression is not something to be simply brushed aside and written off. It is a struggle we must determine to persist in. Struggle is proof that we have not yet been conquered. It is God's plan and purpose for our lives that we might find peace in all of the situations that we find ourselves in. God gave us the Word, not simply for the times that it is easy to read and understand, but for the times that we feel as though we cannot find our next step forward. Find Him, cry out to Him, and rest in Him and you will find yourself on the path to the cross that bears the name of Christ and the redemption that it carries.[11]

TODAY ...

TOMORROW ...

Write down your thoughts, dreams, and hopes.

> Because thy lovingkindness is better than life, my lips shall praise thee.
>
> – Psalm 63:3

The best cure for an empty day or a longing heart is to find people who need you. Look, the world is full of them.

– Anonymous

THE LIE ABOUT BEAUTY

A well-known celebrity is found screaming at paparazzi as she walks the distance from her flight to her ground transportation. This usually friendly star surprises the media as she yells and runs for cover. The reason? She didn't have any makeup on and her complexion is quite bad, according to an insider, so she didn't want to be seen. Hmm . . . why would this popular actress feel the need to hide from us? I mean, it's her talent that we admire, right? Or does even she, with all her wealth, fame, and genuinely good looks know that we are judging her by her face? She knows it and we know it too.

The most alarming truth about this is that if someone that most people would label "beautiful" feels less than that label without makeup on, what hope does that give the rest of us "average" people? Oh, but see what's great about this is that it shows us how ridiculous our obsession with physical beauty is.

The truth is that our culture is obsessed with looks. So much so, that the only women that model clothes and beauty products seem to be around 98% thinner than the average woman! Magazine covers are swarmed with airbrushed (and when I say airbrushed, I'm not just talking about covering a pimple . . . I'm talking about cutting away at the woman's waist and thighs to make them look smaller than they actually are) ideals in order to show us that these woman have it together because they look good!

People, (and I mean ladies mostly) we need to stop the obsession with beauty! It is a waste of our time and a detriment to our self concept. There are very few people out there that would say that they feel great about the way they look, and that is a very sad thing, especially since God makes it plain in His Word that He doesn't give a flying fish about what we look like. It's skin and hair, not heart and soul.

But the Lord said to Samuel, "Do not look at his appearance or at the height of his stature, because I have refused him. For the Lord does not see as man sees; man looks at the outward appearance, but the Lord looks at the heart." —1 Samuel 16:7

I know it's hard not to fall into the mentality and I've struggled with it myself, but I have come to the point where I believe that I am beautiful and it's not because I've perfected the latest makeup technique. It's because God has told me that I am beautiful to Him and I finally started to believe it.

In high school, my boyfriend (now husband) and I started dating when I was a junior. I barely wore any makeup, my hair was quite an undone mess, I weighed more than I do now, and my clothes were not all that impressive because I just couldn't afford it. The money I made at work paid for my car insurance and for any random expenses (going out to eat, buying birthday presents, tithe, etc.). On top of that, I would say that I was somewhat insecure. I kind of liked some things about my personality (like my "I don't care what they think about me" loud mouth even though I really did care) and I even thought I was kind of funny. But overall, I wouldn't say that I thought I was anything special. I had never had a boyfriend, and any boy that had shown interest in me, I had decided did not look "cool" enough for me to date . . . so I remained loveless for most of my high school years.

The crazy thing is that Todd still liked me. Not only that, he pursued me. The reason why this is amazing is because later on I started to develop a desire for looking nicer. I had a friend who always looked perfect and I decided that I too would strive to be like her. She had makeup books and all kinds of cool clothes. I would try too! I'd take my mom's free samples of makeup and work extra long to blow-dry my hair. I'd accessorize and buy a cool shirt whenever I could. This progressed for months and I was loving my new attitude toward my looks. The funny thing is that it's hard to put much energy into one thing and not lose it in something else. What I am saying is that this desire to look good must have impacted my personality negatively because Todd ended up telling me one day, "You know honey, I think you're beautiful, but I kind of liked it more when you didn't really care all that much about what you looked like. That was part of the reason that I was drawn to you." WHAT???? I seriously could not understand what he was saying. How could you tell me that you liked it more when my hair was less tame and I didn't wear contrasting eye shadow? I mean come on . . . this is common sense we're talking about! I look better now . . . you should like me more! That's what society would have liked me to believe anyway.

That day I learned two life-changing things:

1. I had found a quality man.
2. What we have learned about beauty is a lie.

The world is judging us by our looks. That is a fact and if we are honest enough with ourselves we will admit that we do it too. We, however, have the power to change that. First of all we need to stop deciding what people are like without seeing them through God's eyes. Even the most detestable person in our eyes (a murderer, child molester, or someone with a huge deformity) is God's child and someone that Christ went to the cross for. Second of all, we need to stop obsessing with ourselves and feeling down when we look into the mirror. Even more than that, we need to stop looking into the mirror so much! It's perfectly okay to get ready for your day and feel good about the way you look. I am not saying that you shouldn't care about what you look like, but there comes a point when you have to realize that (like most things) your self concept is a heart issue. If you are not feeling filled up on the inside, the outside is not going to look very nice to you. In the mornings I've prayed during my quiet times "Lord make me beautiful on the inside with Your Word, because if I am not beautiful on the inside, it does not matter in the least bit what I look like on the outside." Ever known a beautiful girl that wasn't very nice? She didn't look so good after she looked down on you, did she?

I know that we don't believe the cliché, "Beauty is on the inside" but just like the "Golden Rule" it is true. This is why God makes the statement to Samuel to not judge on the appearance of Eliab. God knew it from the start that people were going to judge based on faces. Knowing this He plainly tells us to stop. His whole Word is constantly reflecting on the condition of our hearts. It says very little about our face and figure.

Let's stop obsessing about our looks. We know that it's what man looks at, but God's opinion is the only one that should matter. He had made us the way He wants us to be and we may be preventing Him from using us in a bigger way by channeling our energy into what we look like versus who we are on the inside. The greatest men and women in history have gone down with legacies of making a difference, not because they were so pretty. Let's follow their footsteps and let God beautify our hearts and intentions. Then, He will transform our outward appearance into something that cannot be improved upon by foundation and powder.[12]

Today ...

Tomorrow ...

Write down your thoughts, dreams, and hopes.

> To appoint unto them that mourn in Zion, to give unto them beauty for ashes, the oil of joy for mourning, the garment of praise for the spirit of heaviness; that they might be called trees of righteousness, the planting of the LORD, that he might be glorified.
>
> – Isaiah 61:3

The best part of beauty is that

which no picture can express.

– Francis Bacon

Fighting WORRY

I have a confession to make. I struggle with worry — over-analyzing what should have happened, agonizing over what is happening, and fretting about what might happen. I know some people are more prone to worry than others, but I think we all struggle with worry at some time or another. And that struggle may be at different levels. Some worry is as little as what your parents will say about a bad test score; some as big as the fear of loosing someone close to you.

I often don't even realize it when I am worrying. I'll be thinking about something I did or said that bothers me and it suddenly becomes something I can't stop thinking about. I just can't let go of it. The word "worry" in the verb form actually means "to choke or strangle." It makes sense. If someone grabs you by the neck, you are only going to be thinking about how to get them off. In that instant, it would be hard to think of anything else, wouldn't it? In the same way, worried thoughts and emotions are hard to shake. They scream loudly, squeezing our minds and hearts, and it's hard to move on until the choke hold is released.

I guess my reason for confessing my own worry is that I have been realizing that it is something that doesn't have to strangle us. Our feelings of regret and anxiety are not from God. In fact, His son died to set us free from them. God has something else in mind for us: "For God did not give us a spirit of timidity, but a spirit of power, of love and self-discipline" (2 Timothy 1:7).

Philippians 4:6-7 says, "Do not be anxious about anything, but in everything, by prayer and petition, with thanksgiving, present your requests to God. And the peace of God which transcends all understanding will guard your hearts and minds in Christ Jesus." What's interesting about this verse is that it doesn't say, "Present your request to God and He will give you what you want." It says, "Present your request to God and He will give you peace." And by giving you His peace, God is allowing you to see things more like He sees them.

For a long time I didn't understand this concept. I was feeling hurt and confused by God not giving me answers when I thought I needed them. Then I realized that prayer isn't just about receiving answers — it's about bringing each situation of life into the presence of God. It's asking God to show you, in every situation, how you can think more like He thinks and act more like He acts. Sometimes it will be as clear as day what you should do or say. But other times change will only occur by drawing closer to God and becoming more like Him.

That passage in Philippians goes on to say, "Finally brothers, whatever is true, whatever is noble, whatever is right, whatever is pure, whatever is lovely, whatever is admirable — if anything is excellent or praiseworthy — think about such things. Whatever you have learned or received or heard from me, or seen in me — put it into practice. And the God of peace will be with you." (Philippians 4:8-9) I don't believe you can just say some words and expect all your fears to go away. Getting rid of worry and replacing it with God's peace is a fight that happens in your mind. You have to choose to take that worry and see it the way God sees it. To do that, you have to know what His Word says about it.

My best suggestion for overcoming worry is take whatever you worry about most and find out God's view on it. If you struggle with worry in a specific area, then read, meditate on, and memorize Scripture about that area. Do a Bible study on the subject. Put verses up around your room or in your car to remind you of what is lovely and excellent. Fill your mind with God's view so that it is available to you the instant you need it! To get you started, I've included a bunch of verses that will be helpful in the battle toward peace.

For I am the Lord, your God, who takes hold of your right hand and says to you, do not fear; I will help you. – Isaiah 41:13

There is no fear in love. But perfect love drives out fear. . . . – 1 John 4:18

Fear not, for I have redeemed you; I have summoned you by name; you are mine. When you pass through the waters, I will be with you; and when you pass through the rivers, they will not sweep over you. When you walk through the fire, you will not be burned; the flames will not set you ablaze. – Isaiah 43:1-2

The Lord is good, a refuge in times of trouble. He cares for those who trust in him. – Nahum 1:7

I will instruct you and teach you in the ways you should go; I will counsel you and watch over you. – Psalm 32:8

I will lead the blind by ways they have not known, along unfamiliar paths I will guide them; I will turn the darkness into light before them and make the rough places smooth. These are the things I will do: I will not forsake them.
– Isaiah 42:16

Yet I am always with you; you hold me by my right hand. You guide me with your counsel, and afterward you will take me into glory.
– Psalm 73:23-24

For God did not give us a spirit of timidity, but a spirit of power, of love and self-discipline.
– 2 Timothy 1:7

So we say in confidence, "The Lord is my helper; I will not be afraid. What can man do to me?" – Hebrews 13:6

God is our refuge and strength, an ever present help in times of trouble. – Psalm 46:1

Peace I leave with you; my peace I give you.
I do not give to you as the world gives. Do not
let your hearts be troubled and do not be afraid.
— John 14:27

Cast your cares on the Lord and he will
sustain you; he will never let the righteous fall.
— Psalm 55:22

Come to me all who are weary
and burdened, and I will give you rest.
— Matthew 11:28

And let the peace of God rule in your hearts,
to which you were called to one body; and be
thankful. — Colossians 3:15

And my God shall supply all your needs
according to His riches in glory by Christ Jesus.
— Philippians 4:19

This passage (from *The Message* translation)
is great for the "little things" we fret about:

If you decide for God, living a life of God-worship, it follows that you don't fuss about what's on the table at mealtimes or whether the clothes in your closet are in fashion. There is far more to your life than the food you put in your stomach, more to your outer appearance than the clothes you hang on your body. Look at the birds, free and unfettered, not tied down to a job description, careless in the care of God. And you count far more to him than birds. Has anyone by fussing in front of the mirror ever gotten taller by so much as an inch? All this time and money wasted on fashion — do you think it makes that much difference? Instead of looking at the fashions, walk out into the fields and look at the wildflowers. They never primp or shop, but have you ever seen color and design quite like it? The ten best-dressed men and women in the country look shabby alongside them. If God gives such attention to the appearance of wildflowers — most of which are never even seen

— don't you think he'll attend to you, take pride in you, do his best for you? What I'm trying to do here is to get you to relax, to not be so preoccupied with getting, so you can respond to God's giving. People who don't know God and the way he works, fuss over these things, but you know both God and how he works. Steep your life in God-reality, God-initiative, God-provisions. Don't worry about missing out. You'll find all your everyday human concerns will be met. Give your entire attention to what God is doing right now, and don't get worked up about what may or may not happen tomorrow. God will help you deal with whatever hard things come up when the time comes. — Matthew 6:25-34 (MSG) [13]

TODAY …

TOMORROW …

Write down your thoughts, dreams, and hopes.

> *Trust in him at all times; ye people, pour out your heart before him: God is a refuge for us. . . .*
>
> — Psalm 62:8

Worry is like a rocking chair. It gives you something to do but doesn't get you anywhere.

— Bernard Meltzer

THE TEACHER

I n the movie *Karate Kid,* young Daniel asks
Mister Miagi to teach him karate. Miagi agrees
under one condition: Daniel must submit totally
to his instruction and never question his methods.

Daniel shows up the next day eager to learn.
To his chagrin, Mister Miagi has him paint a fence.
Miagi demonstrates the precise motion for the
job: up and down, up and down. Daniel takes
days to finish the job. Next, Miagi has him scrub
the deck using a prescribed stroke. Again the job
takes days. Daniel wonders, What does this have
to do with karate? But he says nothing.

Next, Miagi tells Daniel to wash and wax
three weather-beaten cars and again prescribes
the motion. Finally, Daniel reaches his limit: "I
thought you were going to teach me karate, but
all you have done is have me do your unwanted
chores!"

Daniel has broken Miagi's one condition, and the old man's face pulses with anger. "I have been teaching you karate! Defend yourself!"

Miagi thrusts his arm at Daniel, who instinctively defends himself with an arm motion exactly like that used on one of his chores. Miagi unleashes a vicious kick, and again Daniel successfully defends himself from several more blows. Miagi simply walks away, leaving Daniel to discover what the master had known all along: skill comes from repeating the correct but seemingly mundane actions.

The same is true of godliness.[14]

TODAY …

TOMORROW …

Write down your thoughts, dreams, and hopes.

> *He that refuseth instruction despiseth his own soul.*
>
> — Proverbs 15:32

I am always ready to learn, but I do not always like being taught.

— *Winston Churchill*

THE SECRET INGREDIENT

In his article "How 'Average' People Excel," (*Reader's Digest*, 1992), Alan Loy McGinnis tells about how Thomas J. Watson, Jr. discovered this "secret" ingredient to successful living and what happened to him as a result.

Watson's father was founder and long-time head of IBM. But young Thomas was a lackluster student who even needed a tutor to get through the IBM sales school. He recalls that he had no distinctions and no successes.

Then he took flying lessons. What a feeling! He learned that he was good at flying. He plowed everything into this "mad pursuit," as he fondly called it, and gained self-confidence.

Watson became an officer in the U.S. Air Force during WWII. Though not brilliant, he discovered that he had "an orderly mind and an unusual ability to focus on what was important and to put it across to others."

He capitalized on these traits and went back to IBM. He eventually became chief executive of the corporation and took it into the computer age. In 15 years, he increased IBM's revenues almost tenfold.

What is it that some "ordinary" people possess and others lack?

What is that ingredient that catapults some people up and away from the crowd? It is CONFIDENCE.

"It's not what you are that holds you back," says entrepreneur Denis Waitley, "it's what you think you are not." Those who believe that they will never do well in a particular area, probably never will. Those who believe they are not good at anything will forever feel inadequate. But those who refuse to let fearful thoughts hold them back, will quickly excel.[15]

TODAY …

TOMORROW …

Write down your thoughts, dreams, and hopes.

> *For the LORD shall be thy confidence, and shall keep thy foot from being taken.*
>
> *– Proverbs 3:26*

Confidence in the natural world is

self-reliance, in the spiritual world

it is God-reliance.

– Oswald Chambers

I heard a story a few years ago about a farmer in the panhandle of Texas. This farmer and his wife had eked out a meager living in the dusty panhandle for 30 years when an impeccably dressed man in a three-piece suit driving a fancy car came to their door. He told the farmer that he had good reason to believe there was a reservoir of oil underneath his property. If the farmer would allow the gentleman the right to drill, perhaps the farmer would become a wealthy man. The farmer stated emphatically that he didn't want anyone messing up his property and asked the gentleman to leave. The next year about the same time the gentleman returned again with his nice clothes and another fancy car. The oilman pleaded with the farmer, and again the farmer said no. This same experience went on for the next eight years. During those eight years the farmer and his wife really struggled to make ends meet. Nine years after the first visit from the oilman, the farmer came down with a disease that put him in the hospital. When the gentleman arrived to plead his case for oil he spoke to the farmer's wife. Reluctantly she gave permission to drill.

Within a week huge oil rigs were beginning the process of drilling for oil. The first day nothing happened. The second day was filled with only disappointment and dust. But on the third day, right about noon, black bubbly liquid began to squirt up in the air. The oilman had found "black gold," and the farmer and his wife were instantly millionaires.

You have a reservoir of power in your life. If you are a Christian, the Holy Spirit works in your life. You can tap into His power and live your life with resurrection power. The Holy Spirit will empower you to live life on a greater level, but you've got to tap into His power source just like the farmer needed to drill for oil. The Bible says to "be filled with the Spirit" (Ephesians 5:18) and to "live by the Spirit" (Galatians 5:16). People are searching for the power to change their lives when in fact the power is already dwelling within them in the form of God's Holy Spirit. Tap into His reservoir of power! [16]

You will receive power when the Holy Spirit comes on you; and you will be my witnesses in Jerusalem, and in all Judea and Samaria, and to the ends of the earth.

– Acts 1:8

TODAY...

TOMORROW...

Write down your thoughts, dreams, and hopes.

DON'T LIMIT GOD

One of the brightest visible stars lighting the summer sky, Vega, has created a recent stir among astronomers. Scientists think, from very, very long-distance observation (Vega is about 25 light-years or 150,000,000,000,000 miles from earth!) that a large planet might be orbiting this star. Vega itself is about three times the size of our sun and fifty times as luminous, so it's unlikely any life as we know it would exist on the planet.

Less than 20 years ago, no one had ever seen or proven the existence of any planets around any stars. Although scientists have theorized for years that there may be billions of planets in the universe, and perhaps many of them earthlike, no one had ever proven one existed until the 1990s.

Which shows that the more we learn about creation, the more we realize we don't know it all! What a mind-boggling fact to realize He is the One who brings His love and grace to us in Christ.

Everything is possible for him who believes.
– Mark 9:23

Jesus wants you to understand this: never give up. No matter what life brings, always trust God. Refuse to put God in a box limited by your understanding.

Challenge for today: be watchful today for ways to trust God despite all circumstances. Then trust Him! [17]

TODAY...

TOMORROW...

Write down your thoughts, dreams, and hopes.

> *In God I have put my trust; I will not fear*
> *what flesh can do unto me.*
>
> — Psalm 56:4

Before God created the universe,

He already had you in mind.

— Erwin W. Lutzer

ENTRANCE REQUIREMENTS

To become a member of some "kingdoms" you have to meet stiff requirements. Certain organizations and clubs have rigorous standards of acceptance — social, financial, and sometimes racial. If you aren't a multi-millionaire, you don't qualify. Elite universities require nearly perfect SAT scores and high school grades. Corporations demand impeccable credentials before filling executive positions. Very bluntly, they don't want just anyone. Their standards are designed to keep people out.

The good news is that the entrance requirements to the kingdom of God are not that way. They can be met by anyone who opens the door of his life to the gentle knock of the Savior, and by faith lets Him come in. That's because He met the standards of God's holiness for us by His flawless character and obedience to God.

The gospel writer Mark wrote that soon after John the Baptist was thrown into prison, Jesus began to deliver this message: "The time has come. The kingdom of God is near. Repent and believe the good news!" (1:15). Jesus was referring to himself, His work, and the gospel. He was God among men. Soon He would die as the sacrifice for our sins. We can be born into God's kingdom, become members of His family, by receiving Jesus as our Savior.

The good news is also that every one of us — regardless of our social status, ethnic background, poverty, or past behavior — is offered admittance into God's kingdom. It's simply a matter of trusting in Jesus. That's it. No more. Jesus likened it to having the faith of a little child (Mark 10:15).

If you've been trying to guarantee your entrance into heaven by piling good works on top of your good family name and magna cum laude graduate school transcript, forget it. Trust in Jesus. Receive His gift of salvation, and you'll have met every entrance requirement to membership in God's kingdom.[18]

For by grace are ye saved through faith; and that not of yourselves: it is the gift of God.
— Ephesians 2:8

TODAY ...

TOMORROW ...

Write down your thoughts, dreams, and hopes.

During a visit to The Clockmakers' Museum in London, I was impressed to read that many creators of the magnificent timepieces on display were members of "The Worshipful Company of Clockmakers." *What a great name!* I thought. My mind began to race with the idea that perhaps John Harrison, who invented the chronometer, and others like him had acknowledged God as the master of our ordered universe and had been inspired by the heavens. The words of Matthew Bridges came to mind: "Crown Him the Lord of years, the Potentate of time; Creator of the rolling spheres, ineffably sublime."

I was getting carried away when I noticed another document referring to "The Worshipful Company of Blacksmiths," which didn't seem quite as inspiring. A bit of research revealed that the old craft guilds or livery companies of London included "The Worshipful Company of

Bakers," leathersellers, carpenters, launderers, and many others. It was just the name everyone used for these associations of craftsmen, many dating back hundreds of years. My balloon of inspiration had been deflated.

Then it occurred to me that — as a follower of Jesus — everything I do, including my work, should be an act of worship to God. Paul wrote to Christians who were slaves: "Whatever you do, work at it with all your heart, as working for the Lord, not for men, since you know that you will receive an inheritance from the Lord as a reward. It is the Lord Christ you are serving" (Colossians 3:23-24).

As slaves, they had little choice about what they did, but they could decide how they did it. And like them, we can choose to serve Jesus through whatever task is ours today. So why not find a fancy font on your computer and make a sign saying . . .

"[your name] is a member of The Worshipful Company of [whatever you do]" (students, carpenters, landscapers, daycare workers, you name it.)

Every morning when you see that sign, thank God for your task and tell Jesus you're going to do it for Him today.[19]

Be obedient to those who are your earthly masters, with fear and trembling, in singleness of heart, as to Christ; not in the way of eye-service, as men-pleasers, but as servants of Christ, doing the will of God from the heart, rendering service with a good will as to the Lord and not to men.

– Ephesians 6:5-7

TODAY ...

TOMORROW ...

Write down your thoughts, dreams, and hopes.

JUST DON'T FIT?

We've all been there at some point. Like a pair of jeans that have been in the dryer too long, we just don't fit anymore. Maybe we feel this way with old buddies from school or the neighborhood. Our conversation is different, our ideas, our logic, our values. Maybe we dress differently, or listen to different music. It can be frustrating. But what if it's with your siblings or parents — your own family?

I don't have any easy answers. It's difficult to be different from your family, especially when you're living for Jesus and they're not. It's easy to want to distance yourself from them because it's much simpler than to deal with the feelings that build up, or the angry, cutting words that can be hurled your way.

Let me share two ideas that might help. First, ask God to remind you to be an encourager. Don't aggravate them by fighting back. "Live in harmony with one another; be sympathetic, love as brothers, be compassionate and humble. Do not repay evil with evil or insult with insult, but with blessing. . . . For, 'whoever would love life and see good days must keep his tongue from evil and his lips from deceitful speech. He must turn from evil and do good; he must seek peace and pursue it' " (1 Peter 3:8-11).

Second, remember that there is one place where you do fit, and that's in God's family. "You are all sons of God through faith in Christ Jesus. . . . Because you are sons, God sent the Spirit of His Son into our hearts, the Spirit who calls out, 'Abba, Father.' So you are no longer a slave, but a son; and since you are a son, God has made you also an heir" (Galatians 3:26, 4:6-7). Yes, being a believer in Jesus makes you different — but not alone. That's good news and a good fit! [20]

TODAY...

TOMORROW...

Write down your thoughts, dreams, and hopes.

> He that loveth father or mother more than
> me is not worthy of me: and he that loveth
> son or daughter more than me
> is not worthy of me.
>
> – Matt. 10:37

Difficulties are meant to rouse,

not discourage. The human spirit

is to grow strong by conflict.

– William Channing

Swimming to Jesus

The sun was shining on the still water of the pool. Kneeling on the diving board, I peered into the water. The deep end doesn't look that deep, I thought. I can see all the way to the bottom. Without much more thought, I slipped off the board and into the water. As I sank to the bottom, I realized that the water was much deeper than I expected, and it scared me.

That experience was many years ago when I was learning to swim. I had a similar experience, though, when I started college. For me, beginning life as a college student was like jumping into a pool that is much deeper than I had expected. When my parents left me on campus to return home, I had that same underwater feeling of isolation and panic. I thought I might drown.

That first weekend, I went with the Christian Student Union at my college on a fall retreat. On the trip, I was reminded of a recent Sunday school lesson at church. We were reading from the last chapter of John. The disciples had been out fishing all night, but it had not gone well. Toward morning they noticed someone walking on the shore. When one of the disciples recognized Jesus, Peter jumped out of the boat and started swimming toward Him.

As I considered this, I realized how I was panicking about starting college. I needed direction. I needed to look to Jesus and "swim" toward Him. College is a new and intimidating time, but my ultimate focus needs always to be the same: I am to follow Jesus.

So, when you find yourself in a challenging place and think you're going to drown, don't panic. Recognize Jesus and swim toward Him. [21]

TODAY ...

TOMORROW ...

Write down your thoughts, dreams, and hopes.

*And immediately Jesus stretched forth his
hand, and caught him, and said unto him,*

*O thou of little faith, wherefore didst thou
doubt? And when they were come
into the ship, the wind ceased.*

– Matthew 14:31-32

The knowledge that we are

never alone calms the troubled

sea of our lives and speaks

peace to our souls.

– A. W. Tozer

FEARLESS DECISION-MAKING

W hy is it that fear and decision-making so often come as a pair? Confronted by choices — which college to attend, which career to choose (or change to), which words to use to help a hurting friend — making decisions can be a cause of restlessness.

Some of us are reluctant to make decisions because we fear we'll read the wrong sign, take a wrong turn, and head down the wrong highway. We're afraid that our human nature will always skew us toward the "wide path" that leads to destruction (Matthew 7:13-14). As 1 John 4:18 reveals, our underlying issue is the fear of punishment.

Some choices need extra time and care to make, and a little bit of fear is a good reminder of that. But have you ever been so afraid that you couldn't make a decision? During times of confusion, doubt, and worry, I've found these words to be very helpful. Perfect love really does drive out fear:

Afraid of making a wrong decision?
God's sovereignty takes care of that.

Afraid of misunderstanding God's voice?
God can correct.

Afraid of going down the wrong road?
God can provide another on-ramp.

Afraid of the unknown?
God knows it all and understands it well.

Afraid of failure?
God's grace covers all and brings wisdom in the process.

We're not to throw our responsibility for making decisions into the breeze. But fear and anxiety are close cousins, and neither relates well to trust and faith. In Jesus, we are surrounded and enveloped by God's perfect love. We have the freedom to analyze the facts, consult other Christian friends, trust Jesus to guide our decision-making (Proverbs 3:5-6), and take the next step.[22]

T ODAY ...

T OMORROW ...

Write down your thoughts, dreams, and hopes.

> Ye shall not fear them: for the LORD your
> God he shall fight for you.
> — Deuteronomy 3:22

There is a time when we must

firmly choose the course we will

follow, or the relentless drift of

events will make the decision.

— Herbert V. Prochnow

A Man Is Known by the COMPANY He Keeps

Some years ago, the Archbishop of Canterbury was rushing to catch a train in London. In his haste, he accidentally jumped on the wrong passenger car and found himself on a car full of inmates from a mental hospital. They were all dressed in mental hospital clothing.

Just as the train pulled out of the station, an orderly came in and began to count the inmates, "one, two, three, four. . . ." When he saw this distinguished-looking gentleman there wearing a business suit and a clerical collar, he said, "Who are you?"

The answer came back: "I am the Archbishop of Canterbury!"

And the orderly said, "five, six, seven, eight. . . ."

He that walketh with wise men shall be wise:
but a companion of fools shall be destroyed.
– Proverbs 13:20

TODAY ...

TOMORROW ...

Write down your thoughts, dreams, and hopes.

REFERENCES

[1] Brent Porterfield, *Sermon Illustrations*, January 2003.

[2] *Today in the Word*, June 27, 1993.

[3] Stephen Wright.

[4] Craig Brian Larson, *750 Engaging Illustrations for Preachers, Teachers, and Writers* (Grand Rapids, MI: Baker Books, 2002), p. 118, quoting from "Ordinary Heroes" by Ken Walker in *Christian Reader*, Sept/Oct 1995, p. 62.

[5] Craig Brian Larson, *750 Engaging Illustrations for Preachers, Teachers, and Writers* (Grand Rapids, MI: Baker Books, 2002), p. 92.

[6] Craig Brian Larson, *750 Engaging Illustrations for Preachers, Teachers, and Writers* (Grand Rapids, MI: Baker Books, 2002), p. 259.

[7] Peter Marshall, as quoted by Joshua Harris, *I Kissed Dating Goodbye*.

[8] A. Leonard Griffith, *Beneath the Cross of Jesus*.

[9] Neil Eskelin, *Neil Eskelin's Daily Jump Start*® Copyright © 2000.

[10] *Living Christian*, Wednesday, February 18, 2004.